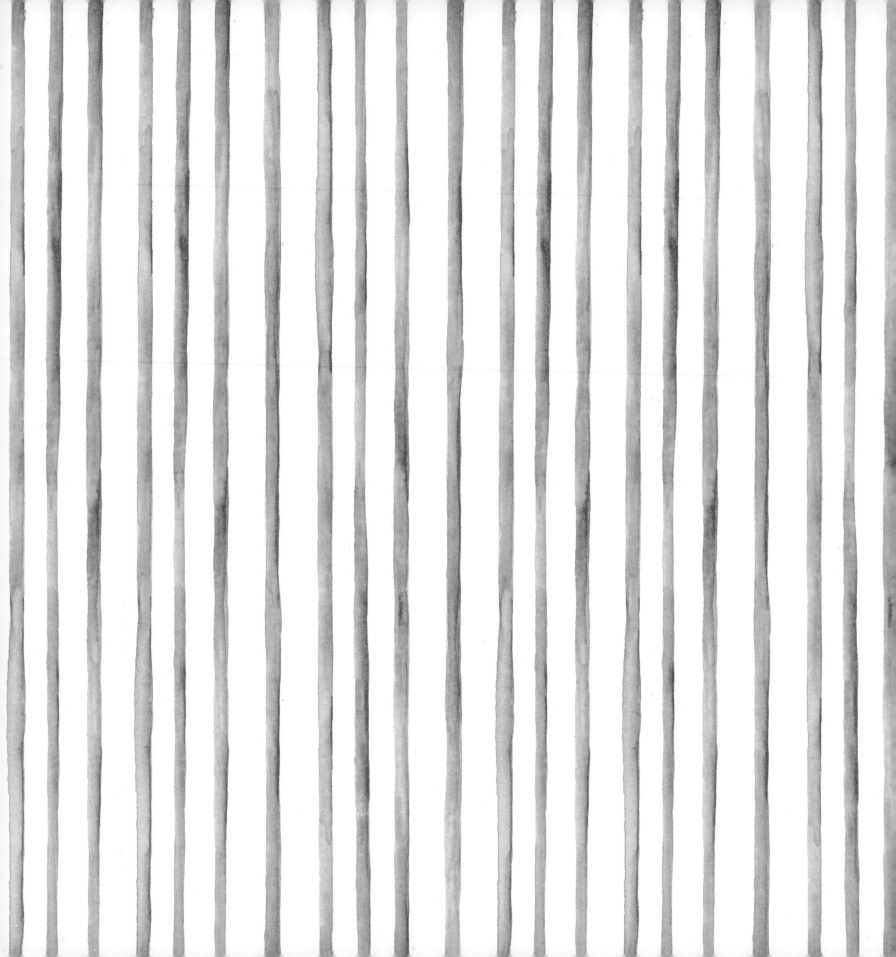

# A LOUD WINTER'S NAP

by Katy Hudson

The Tortoise Guide to NAPPING

Capstone Young Readers
a capstone imprint

A Loud Winter's Nap is published by
Capstone Young Readers
1710 Roe Crest Drive
North Mankato, MN 56003

www.mycapstone.com

Library of Congress Cataloging-in-Publication Data is available on the Library of Congress website.

ISBN: 978-1-62370-869-6 (paper over board)
ISBN: 978-1-4795-9851-9 (library binding)
ISBN: 978-1-4795-9852-6 (eBook PDF)

Summary: Every year Tortoise sleeps through winter. He assumes he isn't missing much. Will Tortoise sleep through another winter, or will his friends convince him to stay awake and experience the frosty fun of winter?

Designer: Aruna Rangarajan

Printed and bound in China.
010599R

Tortoise had just snuggled in for his long winter nap when ...

"Hello there, Tortoise!" chirped Robin. "Would you like to join our singing class?"

"No," grumbled Tortoise. "I was trying to sleep. Tortoises don't like winter."

"Why not?" chirped Robin.

EVERY MORNING

Robin's Winter singing class

Robin

"They just don't," said Tortoise. And he packed up
and left in search of a quieter home.

Tortoise snuggled down in his new bed. He was just about to close his eyes when ...

Tap... Tap... Tap... TAP... Tap... Tap... TAP! TAP!

DO NOT DISTURB (until Spring)

"Hiya, Tortoise! Would you like to make some ice sculptures with me?" asked Rabbit.

"No," groaned Tortoise. "I was trying to sleep. Tortoises don't like winter."

"Why not?" asked Rabbit.

"They just don't," said Tortoise. And he packed up again.

Tortoise trudged through the snow and found a new napping spot. Again, Tortoise snuggled down in his new bed.

He was just about to close
his eyes when ...

"Hey, Tortoise! Would you like to play in our snowball fight?" asked Squirrel.

"No," Tortoise said angrily. "I'm trying to sleep. Tortoises don't like winter."

"Why not?" asked Squirrel.

"They just don't," groaned Tortoise.

"Why would anyone want to stay awake for winter?" grumbled Tortoise.

He was tired and cold and needed to find a quieter place to sleep. Tortoise decided to move to higher ground.

Grown by Rabbit

carrots

Beaver's tools

DO NOT
DISTURB
(until Spring)

Again, Tortoise snuggled down in
his new bed. He was just about to
close his eyes when ...

SWISH
SWISH
SWIIISSSSSHHH!!!

"Oh, no!" cried Tortoise.

DO NOT
DISTURB
(until Spring)

"I do NOT like winter," Tortoise said.

Tortoise hiked up a big, snowy hill.

Behind a small tree,
Tortoise found a flat
piece of wood. It was the
perfect place for napping!

He snuggled down in his new bed and
was about to close his eyes when ...

Whooosh

As Tortoise whizzed along,
he couldn't help smiling.

*Maybe winter isn't so bad?*
he thought.

River

ICE
SKATING

And as he flew off his sled
and through the air, he
couldn't help giggling.

*Maybe winter is more
than cold and snow?*
he thought.

WWHHH HE E

And as he slid across the ice,
he realized he had been wrong.

ˆEEEEEEEEEE!!

That night Tortoise skated, slid,
and spun with his friends late into
the night. He wasn't tired or cold.

Maybe some tortoises could
like winter after all.

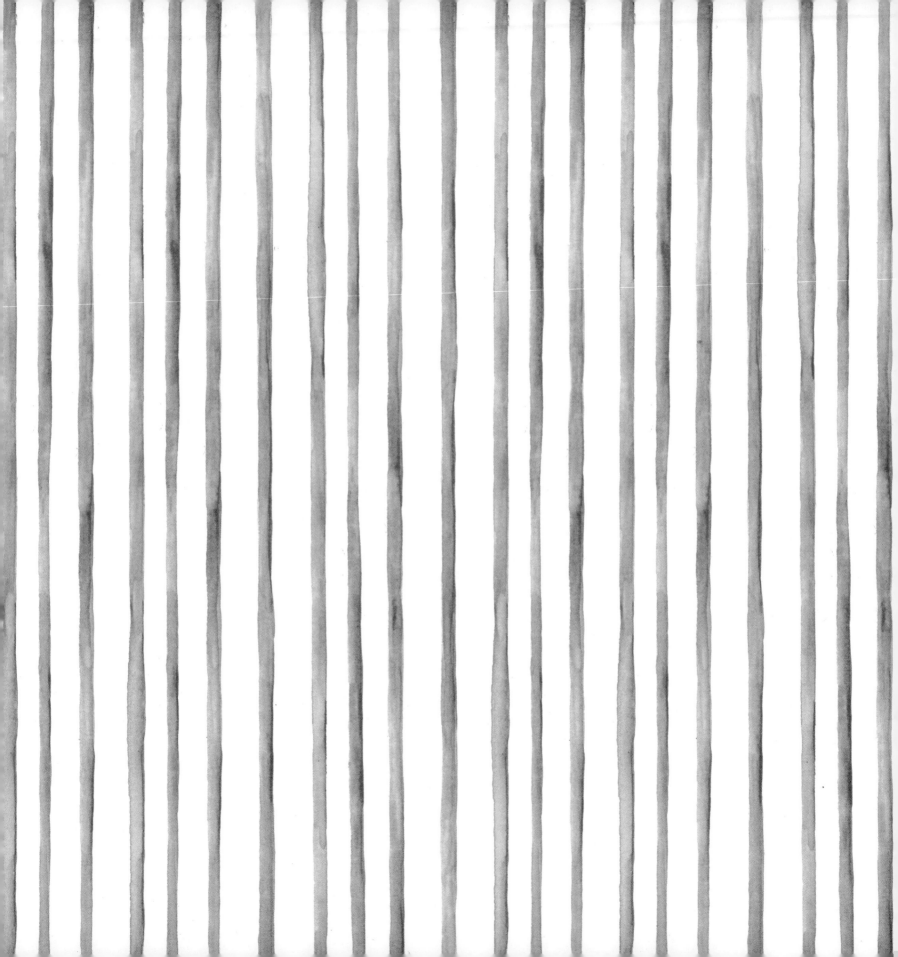